WARNING

This book contains sexually explicit scenes and adult language. It may be considered offensive to some readers. This book is for sale to adults ONLY.

* * * * * * * * * * * * * * * * *

Please store your files wisely where they cannot be accessed by underage readers.

Other books by Shyla Starr:

Persuasive Billionaire BWWM Romance Series

Stacey is trying to keep a handle on her life the best
that she can. She is on the verge of losing her job and
her apartment, while taking care of her sick
grandmother. Her life takes an unexpected turn when
she meets Charlie, who works for the construction
company that is attempting to persuade her to move out
of her home.

Tenacious Billionaire BWWM Romance Series

Adalia is too proud to accept help from the
billionaire playboy, Trent Dawson. How long can she
maintain her resolve? The bank is at her heels to
repossess her business. To make matters worse, Adalia
finds suspicious evidence of Trent's philandering ways.
She must determine whether to trust Trent with the fate
of her business and her heart.

Elusive Billionaire Romance Series

Billionaire Hendrick is trying to repair his
company's image by putting in some volunteer work,
building a school and hospital for the impoverished
children in Africa. There, he meets a beautiful African
American volunteer, Jocelyn. They hit it off right away
but does she belong in his world?

Ardent Billionaire Romance Series

Deirdre doesn't know what to make of the gorgeous
man that seems to be interested in her. His name is
Parker Walters and he seems friendly enough. There is

just something off about him. Why is he trying the hide the fact that he is the heir to his father's billion dollar software empire?

<u>Fervent Billionaire BWWM Romance Series</u>

Alexandra had never been with a white man before. She had seen William at the café before but she always kept her distance. It was unfortunate that their first chance meeting happened when she dropped her breakfast and spilled coffee all over his expensive business suit.

<u>Audacious Billionaire BWWM Romance Series</u>

Chante is torn between staying close to a man beyond her league, and fleeing from him to spare herself from a hopeless position. But she finds she is propelled into a place where she needs to confront her doubts and cast her fate aside to follow the dictates of her heart. Damned if she does and miserable is she doesn't, how will Chante face the events that will lead her to a place of pure happiness or to the pits of a broken heart?

Get the latest update on new releases from the author at:

https://shylastarr.com/newsletter/

This book is Part Three of the "Lonely Billionaire Romance Series"

1 - Love Anew

Tricia was hired to care for billionaire John's wife, who is dying. An unlikely romance emerges after his wife, Rebecca, gives John permission to pursue his happiness after she is gone.

2 - Love Bound

Tricia found herself in another caretaking role. This time, the patient would be her own mother. Her relationship with John was getting complicated. She didn't know whether their feelings for each other were genuine or part of the grieving process from the death of John's wife after a long period of illness. By immersing herself with the task of taking care of her mother, her hope was to forget about John and move on with her life. It didn't hurt that Tricia's best friend's brother, Rod, was a successful and attractive distraction.

3 - Love Decided

John shows up at Tricia's doorstep to finish what they had started. Unsure of what to do but still having real feelings for him, she accepts his invitation for dinner. While at the rodeo with John, Tricia bumps into Rod, the man that she has started to develop feelings for. With two men vying for her affection, Tricia is left with a difficult decision.

Lonely Billionaire Romance Series

Love Decided

Book Three

By Shyla Starr

Copyright Revelry Publishing 2015

Table of Contents

Chapter One

TRICIA WAITED impatiently at the door. Her hands were shaking with nervous tension. It had taken an unbelievable amount of time to do her makeup because her hands kept jerking as she tried to apply lipstick and mascara. Finally, it seemed like it was almost time for John to arrive. Trying to calm her nerves, she sat down on the couch.

Although it seemed like forever ago, Tricia had once been in love with John. Despite their better intentions, they had succumbed to an animalistic desire and had sex—more times than she could count. Tricia had been nursing his sick wife, Rebecca, until she died. After Rebecca's death, Tricia had returned home and taken care of her mother. Now, it seemed like anything was possible. After burying her mother, John had sent her a message and flowers for her birthday. She was going to have dinner with him tonight.

Tricia smoothed her dress awkwardly. She had worn this red dress not long before she had finally had sex with John for the first time. Although she had pretended not to notice, she had seen him watching her slim curves move and strain against the fabric. She cursed herself silently. How could she possibly be trying to dress up for him? Since Tricia had returned home, she had dated Rod. Attractive and successful,

Rod was a wealthy real estate developer. More importantly, he was kind, funny and actually black. Although times were changing, dating someone of the same race would still make her life easier. Ruining things with Rod would be terrible. He was her best friend, Tenaya's, brother and she would probably lose her friend as well as her boyfriend.

Standing up, Tricia walked over to the phone. She wanted to call John and tell him that she could not make it. Being around John would be an impossible temptation for her. Dialing the phone number, she waited until his voicemail picked it up. Unwilling to cancel a date with a message, she went over to the couch to sit down again. Before she could get comfortable, she heard a knock at the door.

Groaning, she managed to smile before she pulled the door open. In front of her, John stood with a handful of red roses. Smiling widely, he made a move toward her and seemed prepared to sweep her off her feet in an instant. Pushing his hand away, she gave him a hug.

Confused, John hugged her before stepping back. "You look... ravishing, Tricia. How are you?" In his voice, she could hear the unspoken question. He did not know about Rod and could not understand her hesitation.

"I'm good, John. For a while, I was confused and depressed after my mother's death. Fortunately, Rod was there to help me through it." As soon as she said this, she regretted it. Tricia had wanted to slip Rod's name in so that John would know she had a boyfriend.

John's crestfallen expression made her instantly reconsider this decision. "Here, come in, come in. I can get you a cup of tea or something before we go. Did you want anything?"

Stepping inside, John seemed at ease finally. Tricia was surprised. With a net worth in the billions, it seemed strange that he should be so comfortable within her small, family house.

John regained his composure and smiled. "Sure, tea would be great. If you have any coffee, that would be even better. I just arrived on the jet and am a bit tired."

Tricia went into the kitchen. As she poured the coffee, she went over what he just said again. Carrying the cups back to him, she set them on the table. "Wait—you just got here? I thought you were here on business. When is your meeting?"

Smiling bashfully, John took a sip of coffee. "Well, that was a little stretch of the truth. Honestly, I just wanted to see you. I had hoped that enough time had passed to be respectful of my late wife so that you would finally date me again. Now, I see that I am a little too late for that." He smiled ruefully. "At any rate, this is a chance to catch up with you and have a good dinner."

Tricia smiled. "That sounds great. I'm sorry about Rod, I just..."

John held up his hand for her to stop talking. "No excuses needed. I completely understand." He finished the rest of his coffee in a gulp. "Did you want to go to that one restaurant downtown? I don't recall the name, but it was this delicious French place in a spinning ball.”

Laughing, Tricia shook her head. “You mean Reunion Tower?” she paused. Rod had taken her to Reunion Tower the first time they had sex. She coughed. “Um, maybe not something so fancy. This is the first time I get to see you again, so maybe somewhere more relaxed.”

He noticed that she was hiding something or trying to avoid going to Reunion Tower, but John was smart enough not to press the issue. “Sure, I have the perfect place. Do you have any cowgirl boots?”

Tricia shook her head. “What? Why?”

Laughing, John led her to his car. From the trunk, he pulled a pair of red boots that were exactly her size. Confused, she looked up at him. “How did you know that I would need them? Or that I would be dressed in red?”

Smiling, John kissed her on the forehead. Instinctively, Tricia leaned her head back for a kiss before she remembered that they were not together anymore. John hugged her instead. Pulling away, his eyes twinkled with amusement. “Well, I rather hoped you would wear red—you look so good in this dress. As for needing them, I figured that you would turn down the fancy restaurant. You're classy, but you’re more in your element in the real world where people care about enjoying life—not gourmet cuisine. At any rate, I figured I'd be prepared.” Pulling out a black pair of boots, he pulled them on as she put her red boots on. Holding open the door for her, he helped her into the car.

Throughout the ride, John refused to say where they were going. As they exited the freeway, she realized that they were headed toward Arlington, Texas. Confused, she glanced over at him. "Where in the world are we going?" she asked.

John shrugged as he turned a corner. "We'll be there in a second and you can see. For the full experience, I was thinking you could escort me to a rodeo in Mesquite tonight. I don't often have time to take in the sights and amusements of Texas. To be honest, I don't think that I have ever been here for anything other than business."

Pulling into the parking lot, John helped her out of the car. She glanced up at the sign. "Trail Dust Steakhouse?"

John smiled. "A client took me here once. I learned the hard way that this is a pretty relaxed place. They cut off my tie when I walked in the door."

Tricia glanced over at him to see if he was joking. "Seriously?"

Laughing, John held the restaurant door open for her. "You'll see, it's a great place, really. There should be some line dancing later on tonight as well."

Following the hostess, they arrived at their table and ordered some steaks. In the middle of the restaurant, a giant slide stretched from the second floor to the first. Children were happily running up the stairs and down the slide. As their drinks arrived, John motioned to the children. "You ever want one?"

Tricia nodded. "Yes, someday. I'm surprised you never had any children with Rebecca."

Shaking his head, John leaned back as the server set a steak in front of him. "No, we never had children. We always thought there would be more time."

Leaning back, Tricia sipped her drink as she gazed around the room. Many of the diners were dressed in western gear. Looking back at John, she picked up her knife to cut the steak. "You know that this is a weird conversation. Even if I were single, it would still be questionable about if we ever had kids. What type of life would a half-black, half-white child have? Where would they belong?"

John shrugged. "They'd figure it out. It isn't the 1960s anymore, you know. Plus, I live in Washington state. Things are a bit more liberal up there than here."

Tricia swallowed her bite. "True, but don't you think we'd have to care? As parents? We should give them the best chance they have at life." She laughed. "You tricked me into continuing this conversation." Pointing her knife teasingly at him, she shook her head. "We are only talking as old friends, John. Remember that."

John motioned to the dance floor. The children were being removed from the slide to make room for line dancing. "Well, old friend, care to dance? We don't even have to touch each other."

Smiling, Tricia consented and allowed him to lead her onto the dance floor. As the music started, she suddenly felt a thrill of exhilaration. It was like her body was finally coming back to life as she danced. Nothing mattered in the world other than the rhythmical pulsing of boots on the wooden floor and the twanging beat of country music flowing through her veins.

Finally, she motioned to John that she had to stop. They had danced for long enough. John smiled at her with his bright, white smile. Putting his hand on her hip, he led her back to the table where he tossed a few 20 dollar bills to cover the cost of the meal. Although she felt she ought to tell him to take his hand off of her hip, she did not want to. It felt so perfect and right. It was like she had spent the last few months just waiting for this moment.

Returning to the car, John started to drive to the rodeo. Tricia placed her hand on his arm. "Wait, stop at a liquor store before we get there. It will be cheaper if we can sneak alcohol in."

John laughed. "Are we in high school?"

Rolling her eyes, Tricia snorted. "No, but us normal people we still have to save money."

Chuckling in amusement, John pulled into a liquor store and waited until she came out with a bottle of vodka. Slipping it between the folds of her purse, Tricia smiled. "That should do it. They don't search too hard."

After pulling into the rodeo, John went to buy tickets and they got into the arena without any issues. Before the event could start, they purchased a couple of cokes and surreptitiously poured several shots of vodka in each. Leaning back, John wrapped his arm around Tricia as they sat down. Again, she felt like she should tell him no and could not. With her head next to his body, she could smell his cologne and make out a few chest hairs sticking out of his shirt.

John winked at her as he caught her looking at his chest hair. "My eyes are up here, darling." He drawled in a fake southern accent.

Tricia laughed again. Already, the vodka was getting to her. "Your accent is terrible, by the way. That's closer to a Georgian accent than a Texan one."

Good-natured, John just shrugged. "Maybe you should teach me. Lay a little Southern charm on a poor northern boy like me." He grinned wickedly.

Pushing him away teasingly, Tricia leaned back as the rodeo started. Rodeo clowns flooded the area and bulls darted across the dirt. She had not gone to the rodeo since she was a child. Tricia had always begged her mom to take her here for one reason. Children under a certain age were allowed to chase after the younger bulls. If they could pull a ribbon off of the bull's horn, the child was given some type of prize. Tricia had never won, but this had not stopped her from begging her mom to bring her here every spring.

Blinking away a tear at the memory, Tricia started to stand up. John glanced up in curiosity. "I just needed to go to the lady's room. Maybe get us some more cokes."

John nodded and stood up. "No problem. I'll get the sodas and we can walk back together."

Entering the restroom, Tricia walked over to the mirror. With the rodeo still going on, there were very few women in the bathroom. She looked in the mirror. Staring back at her was a gorgeous, lively black woman with bright eyes. Surprised, she looked closer at her reflection. This was the best she had looked in weeks. Something was different in the reflection that gazed back at her. There was more life and happiness in her expression. Pausing, she pulled a lipstick out of her purse. She was going to be in so much trouble if she stayed with him for long tonight.

Finally, she left the restroom. Turning the corner, she ran headfirst into Rod. Stunned, she stepped back. "Oh, hi," her voice was unenthusiastic and she immediately cursed herself silently.

Rod seemed taken back. He did not understand why she was not happy to see him. Shrugging it off mentally, he leaned forward and kissed her. Her lips were cool and unresponsive against his. "What's wrong? And what are you doing here, Tricia?"

Awkwardly, Tricia shrugged. "I'm fine. I just came here with an old friend. What brings you here tonight?"

Rod motioned toward the refreshments counter. "Just getting some drinks for an out-of-town developer and me." He waited awkwardly for a moment and started to leave. Before he could, John walked up and handed Tricia a Sprite.

"Sorry about the Sprite, I ordered coke. For some reason, that is not what they heard." Stretching out his hand to Rod, he smiled affably. "Hi, I'm John. How are you doing?"

Rod coughed. He did not like the way this situation looked. Raising an eyebrow, he shook John's hand. "I'm Rod, Tricia's boyfriend. What brings you to town?"

John smiled. "Business, like always." Now he knew who the competition was.

Glancing over at Tricia's silent face, Rod frowned. "What type of business?"

Before John could respond, Tricia pulled at his arm. "We're headed back to the rodeo now. I'll call you tonight, Rod."

Rod leaned forward to kiss Tricia, but she moved so that the kiss fell on her cheek instead of her lips. Both men noticed this movement. Frowning, Rod walked away to get his drinks.

Returning to their seats, John poured another few shots of vodka into the sodas. "So that was Rod, huh? He's pretty good-looking."

Tricia shrugged. She did not like this conversation. Grabbing the cup from him, she downed all of the soda and liquor. "Let's get out of here. I don't want to talk about this."

John stood up. "Whatever you want. Any particular destination in mind?"

Tricia shook her head. "Let's just drive."

Getting on the roadway, they started to drive east. John was silent as he waited for Tricia to say something. Sitting next to him, Tricia just stared out the window. Things were already falling apart and nothing had happened. She could probably fix things with Rod fairly easy, but fixing her own emotions would be harder. It felt like she was standing at a precipice and looking over. If she decided to leap off the edge, she would be unable to change her mind in the future.

Finally, she looked over at John. Pulling out the vodka, she took a swig. John raised an eyebrow. "You kept the rest of the bottle?"

Tricia handed it to him. Sighing, he took a gulp. Noticing a side road, he turned off. Over the last few minutes, they had managed to drive out of the DFW metropolis and were on country lanes. The road they turned onto had no houses in sight. Some oak trees hid their car from the main road as they parked in an empty meadow.

Tricia glanced at John in surprise. "Why did we stop?" she asked.

"If you want to drink, we need to stop driving. I can always call a cab from here later. GPS should make it easy enough for the cab to find us."

Sighing, Tricia glanced at him. As she turned her face, her lips nearly hit his. She did not move a muscle and John remained frozen. Only a centimeter away from his mouth, her lips quivered with anticipation. Long moments passed, but neither person moved closer to the other. Within the car, the sexual tension became thick enough to cut with a knife.

Coughing, John moved his head back. He pulled out the vodka bottle and took another swig. "You are playing a dangerous game here. Maybe I should take you home. If you don't want anything to happen, I'll make sure you get home safe and with a clean conscious."

Silent, Tricia leaned back and closed her eyes. Images of John's body flashed across her mind. In her mental eye, he was behind her and thrusting inside of her. His hands ripped her clothes off. Sighing in frustration, she opened her eyes again. John was still sitting next to her and waiting for her to say something.

Perhaps it was the alcohol or the last year of grief. Whatever caused it, Tricia suddenly felt reckless. Pulling his keys out of the ignition, she tossed them in the backseat. She slid her leg over the top of him and straddled his body. Unquestioning, John pushed his seat farther away from the steering wheel. He waited for her to make a move—he did not want to push her into anything.

Tricia ran her tongue over her lips. Seductively, she leaned forward and whispered into his ear. "Don't kiss me."

Slowly, she brought her lips against his. Only a hair's breadth away from his, he could feel her breath against the soft skin of his mouth. Moving her lips so they remained almost touching his body, she allowed them to trace the outside of his ear and the line of his neck. Beneath her, she could feel John trembling in desire. With only the thin material of his slacks and the lace of her underwear between them, she could easily feel his cock harden against hers. The very thought of him inside her made her maddeningly wet. She wanted to touch him and stroke him, but could not bring herself to break this spell. As long as her lips did not touch his and they did nothing physical, she was not cheating on Rod yet.

She ran her hand along her collarbone and played with her nipple. Beneath the thin black lace of her bra, her nipple visibly hardened. John groaned and thrust his hips upward. With so little fabric between them, his cock rubbed against her clit. Noticing her response, he did it again. Breaking the spell slightly, he grabbed her hips and pulled them hard against him. The stimulation to her clit drove her wild. All she wanted was for him to be inside of her.

John could not stand it anymore. His teeth found her ear and he nibbled along the edge teasingly. Tricia looked down at him in surprise. "But I thought..." she started to say.

Before she could finish her sentence, John pulled her mouth down against his. His tongue moved against hers in a rhythm that she knew very well. Within her, it felt like fireworks or shooting stars were exploding in quick succession. She did not care anymore. Faithful or not, she did not care about anything. All that existed for her in this moment was the thought of John with her and inside of her. Yanking at his belt, she unbuttoned his pants so his throbbing member could break free. Long and hard, it was already dripping pre-cum with anticipation and desire. Slipping off her underwear, she straddled him. John reached for the glove box for a condom, but she pushed him away. If she did not have him now, she would explode with pent-up desire.

The lips of her cunt teased invitingly around his head. He could feel each nuance of her and the wetness that was beginning to surround him. With one quick thrust, he entered her. Again and again in quick succession, he allowed the entirety of his shaft to penetrate her body. Pain and pleasure intermingled in her mind as she cried out. Her screams of pleasure sounded like something out of an ancient mating ritual or an old harvest celebration. Her female nature invited him in as a part of something that had existed since the beginning of time. With each thrust, her body became his and he likewise became a part of her. They were no longer separate beings, but one soul rocking with fervor in his car. The windows fogged up as she moved her hips hard against his. Bringing him close to orgasm, she slowed down again and again to drag him away from the brink. Again, she moved her hips fervently and harshly against his. By the third time John approached orgasm, she could not take it any more. She had to come with him. That was the only way that this desire and union of their souls could be completed. Throwing back her head, she moaned loudly as she came around him.

As she left the pinnacle of her orgasm, Tricia realized it was not enough. She wanted him in every way possible. Just having sex would not be enough tonight. Kissing him passionately, she poured another shot down his throat as she drank an additional shot. She pulled him out of the car and bent over against it. Her long legs rose in a sleek line out of her cowboy boots. With her dress pulled up from sex, the line of her bottom was visible beneath the dress. Behind her, John was sexily tousled. His shirt had come unbuttoned during sex and his hair was a blond swirl around his head. Ripping off his shirt and undershirt, he exposed his naked muscles to the open night air. He no longer cared if anyone drove by and saw him. In his eyes, lust shone through and danger lurked. Stripping off his boxers, he put his manhood against her backside.

"What do you want?" John asked. His voice was strained as he tried to hold his body back from continuing.

Tricia shrugged. "I want you in every way possible. Use me however you want."

John did not need to be told a second time. He touched himself and felt her wetness still around his cock. Using moisture from his mouth, he wet the head further before entering her anally. Unwarned, Tricia cried out. The first instant of pain quickly subsided and she felt a new, different type of desire. Unlike typical sex, this sensation was entirely different. To her surprise, it was not unpleasant. Actually, she liked it. Pushing backward into him, she helped him thrust harder.

The added tightness around him brought John closer to orgasm than he had thought possible this soon. Reaching around to her chest, he fondled her breasts as he attempted to slow the almost compulsive thrusting of his hips. Instead of calming him down, the softness of her breasts and hard nipples made him even harder. Groaning in agony, he leaned back and placed his hands against her hips. Pulling her into him roughly, he tried to get the full length of his shaft inside. Frustrated by his inability to fit fully within her, he tried thrusting again. The tightness just teased him and brought him closer to orgasm without full satisfaction. Moaning in agony again, he ripped her from the car and threw her to ground. Tricia started to say something, but he held his hand over her mouth. There was no way he could stop even for a moment.

Entering her cunt again, he sighed in pleasure as he managed to fit his entire shaft within her. Tricia's wrists hurt slightly as he held her down. His weight was crushing her body, but she just wanted more. Free to talk at last, she whispered, "Hit me."

Without thinking about it, John pulled his hand back and slapped her. Although she did not understand why, this turned her on immensely. She nodded to him again. "Hit me. Harder."

John hit her again. As she started to tell him to hit her even harder, he placed both of his hands around her neck and choked her. The sudden lack of oxygen stimulated her nerves and allowed her to feel each part of her body as he thrust. Nodding her head and unable to speak, her eyes urged him on. John choked her again.

Pulling one hand down from her neck, he fondled her clit. The extra stimulation brought her close to orgasm. Choking and unable to call out, she let out a silent moan as her body shook with her orgasm. Like an earthquake or tsunami, the orgasm passed over her body and caused convulsions within every fiber of her muscles. Above her, John started to orgasm for the second time of the night. Sighing in pleasure, he collapsed next to her.

Rolling against his body, she leaned her head on his chest. He lazily traced his hand along her back. Within moments, they were both fast asleep and naked in each other's arms.

Minutes or hours later, Tricia woke up. For a second, she was confused. Around her was just woodlands and prairie. Looking over, she saw John and groaned. She had tried to resist for at least a while, but resistance was apparently impossible. Sitting up, she shook some leaves off of her arm that had fallen during the night. Next to her, John began to stir.

Opening his eyes, he smiled when he saw her there. Pulling her back into his arms, he kissed the top of her head. "You are amazing, you know," he paused. "Does this mean that you are going to leave Rod?"

Tricia shook her head. In addition to the beginnings of a hangover, she knew she had to sort out the confusion of her life. "No. Or I don't know. You know that it doesn't make any sense for us to be together."

John shrugged. "When does love make sense? Come on, you can't tell me that you experience that attraction or level of sex every day."

Glaring at him, Tricia reached for her underwear. "I don't choose who I am with based on sex." John laughed at how cute her angry expression looked. "Well, it is a factor. For good sex, two people have to be compatible. So it at least indicates something of a non-physical nature." Pulling on her dress, Tricia motioned to the car. "Come on, drive me home. I'll call and tell you how this all works out."

Nodding, he walked to the car and opened her door. "Fair enough, let's go."

Silent again, Tricia got in the car and stared out the window until he dropped her off. How would she possibly explain this to Rob?

Chapter Two

Still a little unsteady on her feet, Tricia turned the key in her door and waved John off. Entering the darkened house, she dropped her purse in the living room. As she turned, her mind processed the shadows in the room. She realized that someone was there. Reaching for the light switch, she turned it on. Rod was sitting there. He was bleary-eyed from waiting so many hours for her to return home. Tricia stood there silently and stared at him.

Taking her disheveled appearance in, he raised an eyebrow. His voice was cool and showed the effort he was making to remain calm. "Who... was... that...?" he spoke evenly and slowly.

Tricia shrugged. There was no point in lying. What he could not guess on his own, her appearance would show. "I was with John."

"Did you sleep with him? Who is he?" The strain of the pain he was filling slipped out as his voice broke. He ran his fingers through his hair.

Tricia nodded. "Yes. I did. He is my former boss."

Standing up, Rod walked over to the window. "You never told me that you guys were," he paused and spat out the remaining words, "romantically involved."

Tricia shrugged. "I wasn't ready to say anything. Last night was not supposed to happen." She tried to shift her feet so that she could see his expression. Frozen in place, Rod just continued to stare out the window.

"Not supposed to happen? I thought you were with me. Hell, I was thinking about marrying you someday. Without telling me where you were going, who you were with or your history with him, you went off with this guy."

Tricia did not say anything. There were no excuses and she deserved this.

Returning to the couch, Rod sat down. "Do you love him?"

Uncertain what to say, Tricia did not say anything. Rod looked at her again. Judgment was in his eyes.

"Do you love him?" he asked her again. His voice was sharp and hid the anger that was boiling within him.

Gazing straight into Rod's eyes, Tricia kept her face emotionless as she lied. "No."

Rod's arm jerked outward and hit a vase. The sound of it crashing against the wall startled both of them. For the first time, Tricia started to feel afraid. Rod stood up and strode confidently across the room. Pushing her against the wall, he stopped her from turning away from him. Beneath his arms, she could already feel painful bruises starting to form.

"Don't lie to me," he hissed. "Do you love him?"

She nodded slowly. Until this moment, she had not been completely sure of her feelings. She did love John. At the same time, she was starting to love Rod. Until this outburst, he had proven himself to be the man she was searching for.

Moments passed as Rod gazed at her in rage. He did not throw anything or make any movements. Instead, it seemed like he was using all of his willpower to control himself. As the threat of violence passed, Tricia squirmed and tried to get away. Inexplicably, the writhing of her body caught his attention. Sudden desire flushed through his body as he remembered their first time in the Dallas hotel.

Grabbing her arms, he threw her down onto the floor. Grabbing her mother's letter opener from the desk, he held her dress tightly and cut it in a straight line down the front. Her smooth cocoa breast popped out invitingly and her dark nipples hardened enticingly for him. Groaning, he ran the letter opener down her body. The sharp thrill of his knife caused her hairs to stand on end. With the rage of just a moment ago, she feared that he would cut her. At the same time, she already wanted him. Tonight, it seemed like her desire was completely unbridled. For the first time in her life, she would sleep with two men in the same night.

Gliding the letter opener down to his legs, he pulled at the lace of her underwear and cut it in a clean motion. Rod tossed the letter opener to the side and stripped off his shirt. His rippling pecs shone in the dim light as he spread her legs. Placing a finger inside of her, he felt how wet she was. His eyes opened as he realized that it would be impossible for all of the wetness to be from her. Rod felt rage burning again within his chest. If John could have sex and come inside of her, he would do the same.

Pulling off his pants, he prepared to enter her. Tricia tried to push him away for a second as she realized that he was not going to put on protection. "Wait," she said, but he cut her off.

"You let some random guy do this. Why not me? I'm your boyfriend." His voice was filled with anger and hurt. Weakly, Tricia leaned back against the ground and let him enter her. The violent thrust was unlike anything she had ever felt. It was as if he wanted her to experience the pain that he was feeling. Despite the intense pain that accompanied each thrust, she found herself experiencing a sensation of pleasure. The smooth skin of his cock barely fit inside her and each thrust was accompanied by a wide range of sensations.

Rod thrust again. His rage was gradually being driven away by desire. Her lithe body moved against his and accepted him deeper inside of her. Pulling her onto his lap, he caressed the soft skin of her breasts and pulled her nipple into his mouth. The pleasure was excruciatingly sweet and he wanted more. On top of him, Tricia thrust her hips down onto his. With each thrust, he filled her completely and drove her desire into a frenzy. Moving rapidly now, she could not bring herself to stop. She had to have him in her. Across from them, the open window started to let in the first rays of sunshine. People walking by would see them, but she did not care. Even if the whole world was watching her right now, she would not stop.

Moaning with agony, she wrapped her legs tightly around his hips. His abs contracted as he strove to push further into her. Biting into his shoulder, she tried to muffle a scream as she felt herself begin to orgasm. The delicious contractions of her cunt teased and tantalized him mercilessly as he finally started to approach orgasm. Crying out, he came with her and pulled her body into his.

As desire faded, Rod uncomfortably moved to pull on his pants. He had not intended to sleep with her and had actually planned on breaking up with her tonight. This was unacceptable to him, but he could not help it. Her sensual, provocative curves were too enticing to resist. Hell, he had almost raped her in his unbridled passion. Blushing, he looked over at her to see if she was okay.

Next to him, Tricia sat stunned on the floor. The afterglow from sex was slowly drifting away and she realized what an unusual position she was in. Deciding to deal with this later, she shrugged her shoulders. She needed to get a glass of water or her headache would be unbelievably terrible. Standing up, the shreds of her dress and lace underwear fell to the ground. Her warm, chocolate skin gleamed with the glow of sweat and sex.

Across the room, Rod watched her. Each of her curves flowed smoothly into her long, athletic legs. Her full lips were matched by a flat stomach that drove him wild just to think about it. Without consciously thinking about what he was doing, he reached down and touched himself. Already, he was standing straight up. So much for controlling himself. As she poured a glass of water, he stripped his clothes off and strode into the kitchen. Positioning his muscular legs behind her, he pressed against her from behind.

Surprised, Tricia turned. "I thought you were still angry at me. What are you trying to do?"

Rod wrapped his arms around her and held her close. He could smell the sweet scent of jasmine and lilacs on her body. "I have no clue what I am doing. My whole life, I have made the rational decision. I went to college to get out of the ghetto and got a real estate license to make money. Right now, I am doing the most irrational thing possible. Yet... I love you. I am attracted to you like I have never been to anyone. And if you let me, I would take you again right on the kitchen table."

Smiling, Tricia turned to face him. His member brushed against her stomach as she turned and she could feel the hardness of each muscle in his body. "Take me then," she said simply without explanation.

It only took a word from her to release his pent-up energy again. Throwing her stomach on the table, he entered her from behind. The instant sensation of pleasure was intense for both of them. With each thrust, he hit her G-spot with an unbelievably intense force.

Arching her back, she pushed her hips deeper onto him. Every time she glanced back, the sight of his muscles bulging and straining against her only turned her on more.

Grasping on the front of the kitchen table, she used her grip to help her propel her hips into his. The sudden movement caught him off guard. With the sudden pleasure, he orgasmed. Gasping, he fell against her body. The heat of his body against hers felt wonderful. Turning onto her back, she wrapped her legs around him and pulled him onto the kitchen table on top of her. Pushing him back inside her, she enjoyed the feeling of him within her. If only life could always be like this. In this moment, there was no confusion and just raw pleasure.

Rod sighed. Propping his head up on her breasts, he gazed into her eyes. Still inside her, he was finding it difficult to focus entirely. Although desire still remained, it had dimmed and his anger had evaporated. "What are you going to do, Tricia?" he asked.

Lovingly, Tricia stroked the top of his head and rocked her hips against his playfully. "I really don't know. I thought everything was over with John or I wouldn't have started a relationship with you. At the same time, I find myself falling for you. I've never been in a situation like this before and I don't know what to do."

Rod kissed the palm of her hand gently. "Do you love me?"

Tricia nodded. "At least, I'm starting to."

Sighing, Rod thrust deeply inside of her. His cock quivered and he felt a sudden urge to have sex again. Ignoring it, he pulled out of her with a sigh. Standing up, he let her see the full length of his body. The visible admiration in his eyes made him smile. "Well, Tricia. Tell me what you want to do. I will wait however long as you want for a decision. No strings attached. If you want to date me in the end, I am fine with that. If you want to marry me, I would also love for that to happen. You just have to tell me what you want and I will do it."

Nodding, Tricia stood up and walked him to get his clothes. Before leaving the house, he put on his clothes. Tricia remained naked. No one would be able to see her in the entryway and she liked the appreciative looks she was getting from Rod.

At the front door, she gave him a long kiss goodbye. "I'll call you, Rod, and let you know." He nodded in response and turned almost sadly away. Rod knew that this could be the last time that he saw her or their life together. The momentous significance of this brief parting floored him. He just hoped that she made the right choice.

Chapter Three

Sitting alone in her bedroom, Tricia smoked a cigarette. She had bought the pack after her mother died, but only smoked one cigarette out of it. Tricia never smoked, but right now seemed like the time to start. She had no clue what to do. Everything felt right with John, but they got glares from older people whenever they went out. Rod was the right choice on paper. He was successful and caring. Although the moment of anger had scared her at the time, the circumstances were unlikely to ever occur again. Leaning back, she let the cool air from the window blow across her body. She had not bothered to put on clothes and the chilly air caused her skin to form goose bumps.

Tricia began to pace the room as she finished the cigarette. She tried to imagine life without John or without Rod. When she realized that one of these options was impossible, she knew what to do. Immediately, she went to take a shower and sleep. She would need her rest by tomorrow.

Tricia waited through security in anticipation. The flight had seemed impossibly long as her excitement level grew. She had no clue how John would react to seeing her. She had thought about calling him in the last week, but had not wanted to ruin her surprise. In her mind, she imagined him sweeping her off her feet and carrying her to bed.

Finally getting into a taxi, she gave the driver the address to John's house. Staring out the window in thought, time suddenly sped up. Before long, she was at his house. Accustomed to entering through the servant's entrance, she walked by the same guards that she had greeted each day that she had worked here. Although surprised to see her, the guards waved her on.

Entering through the kitchen, she caught sight of Stuart, the chef. "Hey, Tricia! What brings you up here?" He motioned to the kitchen table. "Sit down and stay a while."

Tricia shook her head. "I have to talk to John. We'll talk later and catch up, okay?"

Stuart nodded knowingly. "I understand. I always thought there was something between you."

Startled, Tricia glanced back at him. "You knew?"

Shaking his head, Stuart lowered his voice. His demeanor was friendly. "It's okay, love knows no bounds. Plus, John had gone through enough. Having a moment of happiness was good for him." He motioned toward the door to the mansion. "Go ahead. Go see him."

Nodding in assent, Tricia climbed the stairs and walked through the hallways of the house. At John's office door, she paused. Summoning her courage, she entered the room quietly. Inside, John was sitting at his desk with his head in his hands. She stood there for a moment before saying a quiet "hello".

Looking up, John caught sight of her. He stood immediately from the desk and rushed to her. Grabbing her in his arms, he locked her in an embrace. Stepping back, he kneeled on one knee.

"Tricia, you are the woman that I want to spend my life with. When you are with me, the whole world stops and all I see or care about is you. Be with me. Marry me." He kissed her hand.

Stunned, Tricia said the only thing she could think of. "How did you know to buy the ring?"

John shrugged. "I just hoped that you would come. I've been carrying it around for the last week in the hope that you would come," he paused. "So... will you marry me?"

Tricia nodded and pulled him up from his kneeling position. "Yes, yes, I will marry you."

-The End-

If you enjoyed this title, I would appreciate your leaving a review of the book. Good reviews encourage an author to write as well as help books to sell. Good reviews can be just a few short sentences describing what you liked about the book without having a spoiler. If you could spend 30 seconds writing a review, I would appreciate it: you can review this title right now at your favorite retailer.

Here is a preview of **another story** you may enjoy:

Love Disrupted - Ardent Billionaire Romance Series, Book 1

DEIRDRE CLARKE stepped out of her apartment into the hot Los Angeles sun; dusk had fallen, but the temperature still sat near 100 degrees. Deirdre was already running late for her gig, so the sight of her ex-boyfriend Carl standing by her car irritated her even more than usual. She stomped down the single flight of stairs and greeted him with hostility.

"I'm late. What the hell do you want?" Deirdre demanded.

"Can't a man just stop by to see his best girl?" Carl smiled. His green eyes complimented his mocha skin and for a moment Deirdre forgot why she'd put up with his shit for so long. Then she remembered why she'd stopped.

"I guess you'd better go see her then," she said roughly. "And let me be on my way."

"Dee… you know I'm talking about you."

"I'm not your girl no more," she answered, "and I've got somewhere to be."

"Don't be mad, Dee I just came here to check on you… you alright? What about D'Angelo? You two need anything? You got rent covered?"

Deirdre's blood boiled and she met his eyes with a defiant stare. "I don't need a damn thing from you. D'Angelo and I are not your business anymore." Deirdre had been responsible for her younger brother since their mother had gone to prison. D'Angelo was one of the reasons she'd known she had to get away from Carl in the first place. The last thing she wanted was for her brother to see her thug ex-boyfriend as a role model.

"When are you going to understand that you can't buy your way back here?" She glared at him.

"Deirdre, we were together almost our whole lives. I love you. But I'm not trying to buy my way back. I have a business proposition for you."

"I don't need a job, I have two," she snapped, trying to open her car door. Carl blocked her way.

"Its easy money Dee… you wouldn't even know it was here."

"Ah, I see. You think I'll hide drugs or hot shit for you, after all of the hell you put me through? You think I'd take that risk for you and your 'boys'?" She snorted back at him.

"It's just herb, Dee… it's practically legal. And I don't know why you're so pissed at me. Nothing that went down was my FAULT!"

"Our windows were SHOT OUT, Carl. You can stand there all you want and claim it was a random drive-by, swear it wasn't personal, but I'm not a moron! You think I didn't know you'd fallen in with Derrick and his thugs? You think I believed your lies about where all the money was coming from? I KNEW what you were doing, and you just denied, denied, denied.

Until our home was shot up... with my brother inside. Take your shit and get out of my face." Deirdre shoved him out of the way of her car and escaped inside. She checked her face in the rearview mirror, and then prayed she'd have time to fix her make-up before she had to go onstage.

<<<◇>>>

She stood on stage, in her element. As Lou played along on the black grand piano, Deirdre let all of her emotions flow out to the music. The small crowd gave her their undivided attention as she belted out Trouble, Stormy Weather, and Summertime. Her white, full length gown stood in stark contrast to the milk-chocolate color of her skin.

Deirdre couldn't remember a time when she didn't love to sing. When she was still a young girl, before her father left, her family went to church every Sunday. She loved listening to the soloists in the choir and dreamed of one day standing next to them. But they'd stopped going to church once her father was gone. When D'Angelo was born, Deirdre had tried to get her mother to go back, but she'd refused; D'Angelo's father was against the idea. But soon, he was gone too. Looking back, Deirdre was sure that was when her mother started using drugs, though she didn't realize what was happening at the time. Three years ago, right after Deirdre graduated from high-school, Pauline Clarke had been busted and sentenced to twenty years in a federal prison. Deirdre became D'Angelo's legal guardian, though in all honesty she'd raised him since he was born.

D'Angelo was a good kid, especially considering everything he'd been through. And he was the reason Deirdre hadn't fallen into the same kind of traps the other girls in her neighborhood had found themselves in. She hadn't had any kids, she hadn't gotten messed up on drugs, and she didn't take her clothes off for money. Instead, Deirdre worked as a hotel maid and took college courses online. She'd have loved to go to school on an actual campus, but she couldn't afford childcare for D'Angelo and she refused to turn him into a latchkey kid at eight years old. Deirdre worked while he was at school, and then after dinner they did their homework together.

Thursday nights were different. Those nights were all for Deirdre. She had a standing gig at Fuseli's, an upscale jazz club in the Hollywood foothills. The gig paid just enough for Deirdre to afford her stage-clothes, but she didn't do it for the money.

When she finished her last set, Deirdre took a seat at the bar and ordered herself a beer and a sandwich. As the bartender walked towards the tap, a tall, broad stranger signaled his attention. When he returned to Deirdre, he carried a martini with her draft.

"Dee, a kind gentleman asked me to bring you this and wondered if you'd mind some company?"

Deirdre looked up at Steve and sighed. After her encounter with Carl, she was in no mood to put up with anyone's advances. "Tell him thank you, but I can't possibly accept."

"I don't know… this one's pretty hot, Dee… he's the one down there, in the suit."

"Really Steve, I'm not up for it right now."

"Alright, fine…" he answered in a disapproving, sing-song voice.

Deirdre thought the issue was dealt with as she watched Steve approach the end of the bar to deliver the message. The gorgeous blonde man took the martini, rose, and headed Deirdre's way.

"I'm sorry," she began as he approached, frustrated that he wouldn't take a hint.

"No, I'm sorry." He smiled. "Your friend told me you've had a bad day. You sang beautifully… I sent this as a token of my appreciation, nothing more," he explained, raising the drink. "Why don't you enjoy it? It might make you feel better. Or I could buy you something else, if you'd prefer? Right before I return to my seat, of course."

If you enjoyed this sample then look for **Love Disrupted - Ardent Billionaire Romance Series, Book 1.**

Here is a preview of **another book** you may also enjoy:

**Love Renewed - Fervent Billionaire BWWM
Romance Series, Book 3**

OVER THE last few months, Alexa barely managed to keep her life in order. She had started dating Jerome more seriously, but it did not stop her from having feelings for William. Unfortunately, days like today were impossible to avoid. When she first started working as a publicist for William, she expected to collect a tidy sum. What she did not expect was the impossibility of acting normal around someone she was so attracted to. She sighed.

Across the room, William looked up. "What's the matter? I thought you said everything was about to be under control."

Alexa shook her head. "No, everything is fine. I was thinking about something I need to get done around the house," she lied.

William stood up and walked across the room. From behind her, he leaned in closer as he looked over the press releases she was working on. At this close range, she felt the sexual attraction oozing from his body. He ran his fingers through his hair and Alexa wished his hand was hers. She chided to herself... this was ridiculous. Everything was going so well with Jerome. If she wanted to stay faithful, she would need to leave now.

Abruptly, she stood up and shut the laptop screen. She turned around to come face-to-face with William. He waited for her to say something that could explain her sudden movement. At this close range, she could kiss him if she wanted to. His lips were so close to hers...

"I need to leave," she explained as she tried to fumble with the zipper on her backpack. "I will send you the finished press releases later tonight. We should be able to finish this over e-mail or the phone."

Confused, William nodded. He had no clue why she was acting so strange. Although he knew she had a boyfriend now, he never did anything to imply any non-chivalrous intent. "That's fine. Just send it to my personal e-mail account. If I don't answer right away, shoot me a text message and I'll get to it right away."

After driving around for a while, Alexa was able calm down enough to go home. She was taken. No matter what happened, she had to remember that fact. As she entered the apartment, she repeated this basic fact over and over in her mind. It did not matter. Despite her best efforts, the very thought of William aroused her.

Glancing at the clock, Alexa decided she could give in to her urges just this once. She would go home, run a bath and spend some time fantasizing about William. Having fantasies about him was not out of the question. Plenty of women fantasized about other men without acting on them. She frowned.

A sudden vibration surprised her. Reaching down, she realized her phone was buzzing. It was William.

Flipping to the message with her fingers, she tried to read what it said while she pulled into the garage.

You left only moments ago, but I miss you already. I think I may have sent off the press release by mistake.

She groaned. Despite the cuteness of his message, William created additional work for her. Shaking her head, she messaged him back.

Don't touch anything. I'll fix it on Friday. :).

Exiting the car, Alexa climbed the stairs to her apartment. She unlocked the door and threw off her purse. Finally, she was home. Wandering into the kitchen, she poured herself a glass of wine. This would be perfect. She would start with a glass of wine, fill the tub and relax.

Turning around, Alexa dropped her wine glass. Standing in front of her was Jerome. Her mouth fell open as she tried to think of what to say.

Jerome shuffled his feet in an awkward manner. Now that she arrived home, he felt bashful and did not know what to say. Pulling the flowers out from behind his back, he held them out to Alexa. "I thought I would surprise you," he whispered as he gave her a hopeful smile.

Alexa grinned. "This is so sweet. What's the occasion?" she asked.

He shrugged. "I figured you needed something to brighten your day. You've been working with that one client so much lately that I never see you."

Alexa felt a pain in her heart. He had waited for her with the intention of surprising her. Jerome was so sweet and she had spent the last few minutes fantasizing about William. Smiling, she took the flowers and tried to hide her guilty expression. "That's amazing. It's supposed to be over by Friday, so I'll have some extra time to spend with you, Jerome."

If you enjoyed this sample then look for **Love Renewed - Fervent Billionaire BWWM Romance Series, Book 3**.

Here is a preview of **another story** you may enjoy:

Love Endured: Tenacious Billionaire BWWM Romance Series, Book 3

ADALIA SAT beside the infinity pool at the Grace Hotel and looked out over the deep blue ocean. Trent was inside, a quick business call to sort out his affairs before their honeymoon got into full swing.

She sighed and a smile parted her lips at the taste of salty sea air. Santorini, Greece had been her choice. The quaint white structures and sloping stairs, the city tucked against the mountain, built from the rock itself, was her idea of a fairytale.

They'd arrived a few hours ago and she itched to go out and explore, but there were matters to attend to before they could go anywhere. It irritated her that Trent took the business calls for the bakery, while she didn't have a true business of her own.

One day, she'd be the one in the expensive hotel room, making the calls, buying and selling and checking in on progress. At least, that was her dream.

"You're quiet, my love," Trent said, strolling from the cool interior and taking a seat beside her. He'd opted for an open neck cotton shirt and white pair of slacks. His tan biceps bulged to free themselves from the sleeves restraining them.

Adalia swallowed, overcome by desire again. Every day with Trent was different, an adventure, but one thing would never change – her need for him.

"How was your call?" Adalia asked, squeezing his hand in hers.

"Oh fine, fine. Just some news on the space frontier. We're going live with the IPO in a couple months, so things are going crazy."

"IPO," she repeated, wriggling her eyebrows. "You're opening the company to trade?"

"It's the next big step. We should've done it years ago. Take a look at SkyLyft. They're trading and apart from the debacle with the crash, they're doing pretty damn well." Trent scratched his chin with the tip of his index finger. "But do you really want to talk business, gorgeous?"

"I want to do many things. Including you," she quipped.

He chuckled and picked up a bottle of champagne from the poolside table. He poured for both of them, then handed her one.

"I think we're overdue for a toast after all the shit we've been through," Trent said, then clinked the rim of his glass against hers.

"I couldn't agree more." She raised the flute to her lips. Nausea bubbled in her stomach and she pulled it away again.

"What's wrong?"

"Nothing… I just feel a little strange. I'm fine, really, don't worry." It was probably the plane food.

They'd served some kind of exotic Indian dish and it hadn't gone down well.

Trent slid his arm around her shoulders and pulled her close. He leaned his head against hers and they looked out over the ocean together. "I couldn't have chosen a better destination myself."

"Oh please, you would've had us hiking in Machu Picchu," she said, then pressed a hand to her stomach. Man, the last thing she needed was to start their honeymoon going down on the toilet. That would almost be as bad as DeShawn's attempt to discredit her at the wedding.

Trent's eyes glistened in the morning light. He tipped his head back and soaked up the sun.

Bile crept up Adalia's throat and she stood abruptly.

"What's wrong?" Trent rose immediately and stroked his fingers down her spine.

"I don't know. I just don't feel well." She managed to stand before the nausea completely overwhelmed her. She slapped her palm across her mouth, turned and sprinted for their room. She crashed through into the pristine white suite and grimaced at the off chance she'd let loose before she hit the bathroom.

Adalia skidded around the corner and slid into the bathroom. She didn't have time to close the door. She crouched over the toilet and let breakfast, dinner and what had to be every meal she'd ever eaten present itself in reverse order.

"Oh god, Adalia," Trent hurried into the bathroom and stroked her back. "It's okay, I'm here."

She didn't have the strength to wave him away. So much for romance on their honeymoon. She spent another two minutes in the same state, then flushed the toilet and collapsed against the wall.

Why was everything white in this damn place?

Trent handed her a couple squares of toilet paper and she dabbed at the corners of her mouth. "I'm sorry," she mumbled, "I didn't expect that to happen."

"Don't say sorry, Adalia. It's not like you can help it. I'm worried about you… this looks like food poisoning. We should go see a doctor." He cupped her cheek in his palm and tilted his head to the side, bright blue eyes brimming with concern.

Adalia could barely lift her head. She was exhausted and sweaty, and God, she just wanted a glass of water and a good sleep.

"Don't be ridic –" She pushed him back and vomited noisily into the toilet again. Where could all this have come from –? She'd surely puked out everything else.

"That's it. We're going to see a doctor." Trent rose and hurried into the living room.

Adalia flushed again and struggled into the standing position, then shuffled to the sink. She grasped her cheeks and slapped them to take away the numbness. What the hell was this?

She'd read an article once about eating yogurt to get the local bacteria when visiting a new country, but this was insane. She'd hardly had a chance to unpack. Hell, she'd eaten nothing since they'd arrived, not even a sip of damned champagne.

Adalia brushed her teeth, then washed her mouth out and gargled. That would have to do for now – there was no helping the clammy hands and weak knees.

Trent appeared in the doorway. "Are you done?"

"Yeah, I'm okay. Trent, we really don't need to go to the doctor. It's just a bug… it will pass."

"Like hell it will. Let's go. There's a doctor just around the corner." He guided her from the bathroom with a smile and a gentle caress in the small of her back.

Dr. Michelakis had a moustache to rival Yosemite Sam, and deep brown eyes which expressed a lot of sympathy. He tugged on one of the face caterpillars and leaned forward.

"What's the problem?" he asked, in his thick Greek accent.

Adalia leaned back in the plastic chair at the front of his desk and laid her hands over her belly. "I've got a tummy bug or something. I keep throwing up and I feel a bit sweaty and weak."

The good doctor squeaked back in his chair and studied her, gaze sweeping over her belly and then to Trent.

"Alright. We take urine and blood sample, then we check to see the problem."

"How long will it take until we know what's wrong?" Trent asked, grasping Adalia's knee and running his thumb along the outside of her thigh.

"Maybe hour or two. Our lab is empty of samples now, so should go very, very quickly." Dr. Michelakis rose and walked to the door. He opened it and shouted something in Greek, then walked back to his desk. "Nurse is coming now to take your blood sample." He slapped a plastic receptacle onto the table and smiled at Adalia. "You make a pee in this one now."

What a charmer. She nodded to him and snatched up the plastic container, then hurried out of the room and to the restroom across the hall. Five minutes later, she was back in his office with a vial of yellow fluid. A nurse was waiting, holding a needle and a syringe.

"Is this really necessary?" she asked. "It's just the flu or stomach bug."

"Just let the nurse do what she has to do, Adalia," Trent advised.

She shot him a venomous look. He wasn't the one who had to get holes poked in him by a trigger happy Greek nurse with a nose that could've climbed trees.

The bloodletting was done in another fifteen minutes and Adalia settled in to wait. They'd decided to hang around in the doctor's office. Actually, Trent had decided they weren't going anywhere until they knew what was wrong with her and how to fix it.

"You're blowing this out of proportion," she grunted. "So what if I have food poisoning? I'll throw up a couple times and stay in bed for a day or two. It's not a big deal."

"Of course it's a big deal," he snapped, "I want you to enjoy our honeymoon, not be confined to the bedroom. At least not under this pretext. God, Adalia. Don't you care about your own health?"

"Don't start on me, I'm not in the mood," she said.

The office was empty. The doctor had popped out to catch a quick lunch. Apparently, things moved slowly in Santorini, and his afternoon was clear except for the blood and urine tests.

She grabbed the bottle of water Trent had bought for her and unscrewed the cap. She swigged a few gulps then pulled a face at the resurgence of nausea.

"What is it? Do you need to go to the bathroom? Are you going to throw up again?" he rattled off the questions in rapid succession.

"Oh my God!" Adalia slammed the bottle onto the table top. "Would you fucking relax? You're starting to get on my nerves now."

"I'm just looking out for you," he said, his tone turning sullen. He looked out the window and silence fell between them.

Oh well, it was better than constant questions and concerns. She'd never seen him this way before. He was terrified for her safety, yet there was nothing seriously wrong with her. Trent had revealed a different side to himself, a more vulnerable side. Maybe if she hadn't been about to toss her cookies all over the desk, she would have found it endearing.

The door cracked open behind them and Trent straightened and turned. Adalia stared dead ahead, seething for God alone knew what reason. Because Trent cared enough to rush her to a doctor? That was a good trait, so why did it piss her off this much?

"Ah good, you still here." Dr. Michelakis entered and bustled to his desk, carrying a brown folder and a moustache coated in bread crumbs. He took a seat and brushed the remains of his lunch away from his lips.

"So, what's the verdict?" Trent asked, before Adalia could say a word.

"Yes, what's wrong with me?" Adalia followed up, casting another expression of irritation at her husband. What a way to spend their first day as a married couple.

"Is very simple. I look at the urine sample first and find out the result, but want to confirm with blood test." The doctor opened the file and slid two pieces of paper onto his desk. He positioned his elbows on the wood surface, balled up his fists and pressed them into his cheeks while studying the results.

"And that means what?" Adalia tapped her foot impatiently. She wanted to get home and nap as soon as possible.

"It means what I suspected. You are going to have a baby." He spread his arms wide, then made a cradle and rocked it from side to side. "Congratulations. Such a lovely surprise."

"What?!" Adalia spat. "You're kidding, right? I'm pregnant? I'm getting sick because I'm pregnant. Is this some kind of joke?"

"No joke. You no worry, this is good news for you. Good news about little baby." Dr. Michelakis stood and gestured to the door.

Adalia couldn't bring herself to stand. "I'm pregnant."

"Yes, now have good afternoon. You take the vitamins." He scratched out a prescription on a piece of paper and handed it to Trent. He accepted it, expression completely blank.

Adalia's mind was a mess of emotions and thoughts. How was this possible?

She didn't look at Trent all the way to the drug store. They got back to the hotel and she walked into the bedroom and closed the door, then climbed right into bed, gripping her stomach.

If you enjoyed this sample then look for **Love Endured: Tenacious Billionaire BWWM Romance Series, Book 3**.

Here is a preview of **another book** you may also enjoy:

Love Invested – Persuasive Billionaire BWWM Romance Series, Book 1

"**THEY'RE ASKING** for the eggs to be cooked again."

"What? Those are fine!"

"What do you want me to do about it, Brad? The customer is complaining. Just make them again, alright? He wants the eggs overcooked, apparently."

Brad took the plate from Stacey's hand and returned to his grill, grumbling loudly. Stacey wiped the sweat from her brow and turned around, getting ready to head back out onto the floor of *Papa's Grill and Diner*.

It was the middle of the day in mid-summer, which made the sweltering kitchen unbearable. Stacey was glad to leave the kitchen even if it meant dealing with a couple of jerk customers.

Back in the dining area, she looked around. She had only one couple in her section. They were older, with their shoulders hunched over and beady eyes pointed toward the kitchen. The woman hadn't touched her sandwich, probably waiting for the man to get his eggs back before digging in.

There was only one other waitress, Maria, working, and she was in the corner, texting on her phone. Their place wasn't exactly the hot spot of the city to eat during the best of times. During mid-day, it was more like a graveyard.

The woman motioned for Stacey to come over. She clenched her jaw, exhaled slowly and got ready for whatever ridiculous request the woman was going to make. This couple had been a hassle from the moment they were seated.

"How can I help you?" she asked, plastering a smile on her face.

The woman scowled, "Where are my husband's eggs?"

"They're making him a fresh batch right now."

"Tell them to hurry up!" the woman snapped.

The husband sat there silently, playing with the edge of his napkin. But he nodded at Stacey as if to tell her he better get his eggs soon.

Stacey scurried back into the kitchen. It was mind-numbing if she let it get to her. How long had she been working here now? Four years? It was supposed to be a pit stop before she moved onto bigger and better things. She had been there, scraping by, instead of returning to college or working on making something more of herself.

No use in thinking about that now.

Brad handed her a plate of freshly cooked eggs. She walked back to the table and placed it in front of the man and his wife.

The man wrinkled his nose and said, "This will do, I suppose."

Stacey clasped her hands together and inquired as politely as she could muster, "Would you like more coffee?"

They grunted, and she gave them a fresh pot, making sure not to add it their bill. She was sure they would want something for free out of the egg fiasco. By the time the couple left, Stacey was ready for a break.

In the break room, she slipped off her shoes and rubbed her feet, wincing. Her shoes were cheap, and it showed after standing in them for more than a couple of hours. Her feet were killing her.

She checked her phone next. There was a voicemail from her sister. It was a rare event that her sister reached out to her and she was filled with dread listening to the message.

"Stacey, hey. It's your sister, Allison," she added for clarification as if Stacey wouldn't know her own sister's name. "Listen, call me when you can? I have a question to ask you. Well, more of a favor? But I need to talk to you first. Thanks, bye."

Stacey sighed as the message ended. Her sister wanting a favor never led to anything good. *If she wants money, she can forget it*. There was no cash to give Allison. There were barely any funds for Stacey.

A small TV in the break room played the news. The image was grainy but she could just make out the weatherman talking about rain later on in the evening. *Great.* She made a mental note to make sure the roof didn't leak all over everything when she got home from work. Last time it stormed, Stacey had to set out buckets to catch the drips.

She closed her eyes just for a moment. If she left them closed for too long, she would fall asleep on the spot. It felt as if there was always something to do. She finished one thing, and another task popped up in its place. Maybe that was how it would always be.

"Wake up, sleepyhead."

Stacey opened her eyes to see Amanda stepping into the break room.

"You work today?" Stacey asked, surprised, wondering why they needed another waitress working during such a slow day.

"Nah, I left my wallet here last night in my locker. I was so tired after closing, it just slipped my mind." Amanda walked over to her locker and glanced back at Stacey. "You okay?"

"Yeah, just tired."

"Looks dead here. I'd be tired too," Amanda remarked as she opened up her locker.

"Yeah, it's pretty boring."

Amanda paused in front of her open locker, grabbed her wallet, and tucked it into her purse. When she turned back around, she had a strange look on her face. Stacey sat up straighter.

"What?"

Amanda hesitated and then sat down on the wooden bench. Stacey could see the purple circles under Amanda's eyes. Although they both worked full time at the restaurant, Amanda also attended college. She was probably just as tired as Stacey.

"I heard something. Probably just a rumor. I don't know. I wasn't going to tell anyone but—"

But I know how much you need this job was the unfinished thought there.

"What is it?"

Amanda lowered her voice, "Heard at a class yesterday this place might close down."

"Who was talking about that in your class?" Stacey scoffed. "Especially about our little place."

"Well, I mentioned that I work here. I was in my accounting class, and we were doing a project. This kid in my group said that I should look for other work because this place is going to shut down. Especially with all those investment groups coming in here trying to revive the area."

Stacey scowled. Her neighborhood, which was predominantly black, had indeed been crawling with rich white men in suits lately. All of them wanted to knock down and rebuild her section of town. They wanted to make it new and fresh again. They wanted it to appeal to the elite, which naturally meant getting rid of anyone who was low income.

"Thanks for the heads up, Amanda, but one kid in a college class saying we're going to close doesn't mean we are going to."

"Maybe. But this place is always dead. How long do you think we can stay open like this?" She stood up. "Don't tell anyone I told you, okay? I'll see you later."

Stacey watched her go, suddenly feeling wide awake. Even though she had sounded confident to Amanda that they weren't going to close, the girl had a point. Business had been awful lately. How long would they really be able to stay open?

Maybe it was time to find another job. The only reason Stacey had stuck around there for so long was how flexible the hours were. Few places would accommodate Stacey like that. But if this place was going to close, she may have to put some applications out.

She sighed and rubbed her forehead, fending off a headache. Just another worry to add to her long list.

If you enjoyed this sample then look for **Love Invested – Persuasive Billionaire BWWM Romance Series, Book 1**.

Other Books by Shyla Starr

- Persuasive Billionaire BWWM Romance Series

- Tenacious Billionaire BWWM Romance Series

- Elusive Billionaire Romance Series

- Ardent Billionaire Romance Series

- Fervent Billionaire BWWM Romance Series

- Audacious Billionaire BWWM Romance Series

Get the latest update on new releases from the author at:

https://shylastarr.com/newsletter/

About the Author - Shyla Starr

Shyla currently specializes in writing interracial romance stories and is a huge fan of the alpha male. Simply put, there just aren't enough stories about mixed couple romances, which is something she is aiming to fix.

Being a bookworm all her life, when Shyla discovered men she also realized how easy it was to fulfill her fantasies through her writing.

When not writing and fantasizing about men, Shyla enjoys dancing, reading and chilling with her friends.

Connect with Shyla Starr

I really appreciate you reading my book! Here are my social media coordinates:

Friend me on Facebook:
https://www.facebook.com/shylastarrauthor

Follow me on Twitter: https://twitter.com/shylstarr

Check me out on Goodreads:
https://www.goodreads.com/author/show/8436084.Shyla_Starr

Subscribe to my newsletter:
https://shylastarr.com/newsletter/

Visit my website: https://shylastarr.com/